Alex Wharton

Alex Wharton is an award-winning poet, writer, author and performer, and the Children's Laureate Wales 2023 - 2025. His first collection of poetry, *Daydreams and Jellybeans* (Firefly Press, 2020), was shortlisted for the Lollies laugh-out-loud poetry award and the Wales Children's Book of the Year. His second collection, *Doughnuts, Thieves and Chimpanzees* (Firefly Press, 2023), a lively 'how to' of poetry, rap, haiku and more, is nominated for the Yoto Carnegie Medal 2025. And his third collection, *Red Sky at Night, Poets' Delight* (Firefly, 2024) is the companion volume to this new collection!

Ian Morris

Ian Morris is a passionate illustrator with an authentic voice and is a lecturer at Manchester School Of Art on the Illustration with Animation course. Ian's debut picture book *The Library Book* was longlisted for the Klaus Flugge Prize 2022, nominated for the Yoto Carnegie Illustration Medal 2023 and also endorsed '*Glorious*' by Chris Riddell.

Red Sky in the Morning
Poet's Warning

First published in 2025
by Firefly Press
25 Gabalfa Road, Llandaff North, Cardiff, CF14 2JJ
www.fireflypress.co.uk

A CIP catalogue record of this book is available
from the British Library.

ISBN 9781915444806
ebook ISBN 9781915444813

This book has been published with the support of
the Books Council of Wales.

Typeset and design by Becka Moor

Printed and bound by CPI Group (UK) Ltd,
Croydon, Surrey, CRO 4YY

Red Sky in the Morning
Poet's Warning

ALEX WHARTON

Illustrated by

IAN MORRIS

Firefly

CONTENTS

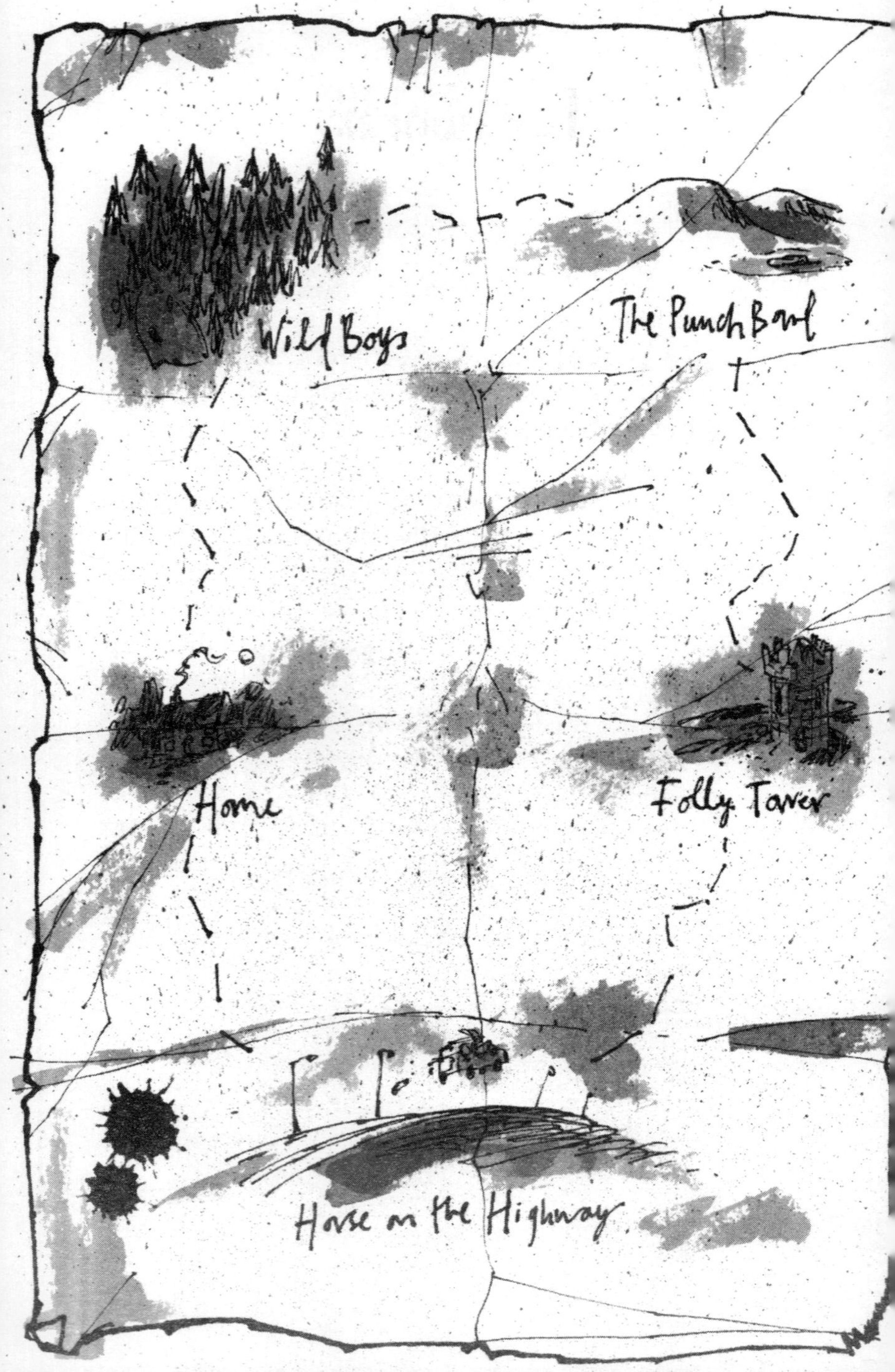
Wild Boys
The Punch Bowl
Home
Folly Tower
Horse on the Highway

Foreword

Okay, this is MoNuMeNtAl NeWs! You've got the book! What book? I hear you ask...THIS ONE! Good grief. You should know. The one with all of the brain-tingling poems in. From wild boys wandering the woods to Welsh wolves with prying eyes, that sneak up close and snatch your...

Wait! I can't give you all the information here. You must travel inside, find a poem that stirs your thinking. Something dangerous maybe, or something dreamy. It's all there, trust me, I wrote the stuff! And much of it I've witnessed myself. Some poems aren't true. Fair enough. I made them up. Well, that's what imaginations are for! You can choose what to believe. But all of them, and I mean every single one, has an energy of its own, and that's important. They are like living things. So, if you enjoy writing poetry or rap or songs, whatever it is, remember to sprinkle some of your own energy upon them. After all, it's you, it's definitely, wholeheartedly, fantastically YOU that will make your work unique. And I (Alex Wharton) solemnly declare that I believe in YOU. Stay Creative. Stay Inspired, Stay Well, Stay True.

So, the part where I solemnly declared how cool I reckon you are, was supposed to be the last bit. But I forgot some important things. I meant to say, R*ed Sky In The Morning: Poet's Warning* is my fourth book of poetry for children and young people (It's for everyone else too). You might have read my third book *Red Sky At Night: Poet's Delight*, If you have, then thank you. If not, then shame on you! Hey … I'm joking, I promise. But I thought you should know that they are companion books. And this one leans more towards subjects of warning, to reflect the title. It's a wickedly wonderful and weird world out there. You'll find all sorts of subjects inside – so go on, get on with it…

Wild Boys

Wild boys in
the wild woods. Lost boys.
Been there for years.
Mad boys. Eyes like
wolves. Run boys, hunt boys.
I saw one; it's true. They
do exist. A single eye
peering from behind a tree.
He followed me. In the
shadows. Behind-bramble.
Tree to tree. I wasn't
scared. They must know
who enters their forest!
Their home! Wild boys.
Lost boys. Running like
wolves. And hiding, like
those who do not want
to be found.

I Don't Want To Write a Poem.

I don't want to write a poem
if it won't be any use,
to a lion or a chicken
or a tiger or a goose!

I don't want to write a poem
if it doesn't want to fly,
every word should be a bird
that tells a story in the sky.

I don't want to write a poem
if the words are fast asleep,
I need fizzy-dizzy-disco-words
that bounce along a beat.

I don't want to write a poem
if it's too afraid to sing,
if the poem has no voice –
then it doesn't mean a thing.

I don't want to write a poem
if there's no imagination,
when we think outside the box
there really is no limitation.

I don't want to write a poem
if it doesn't feel like me.
Creative electricity,
the magic and the mystery.

Where Water Flows

Away from quarrels, worries and woes,
I go to where the water flows.
I go to where the water spouts,
bubbling, gurgling, spilling out.

I wonder where the water's been,
inside of oak and evergreen.
Inside the gut of sheep and horse,
nowhere it's never been, of course!

And all it does is all it knows,
away from quarrels, worries and woes.
I go to where the water flows,
I go
I go
I go.

Time

The more I think
the more I find,
it's how this poet
spends his time.
The cost of time,
I think a lot,
depends just how
much time you've got!
Creating is a magic
thing. Ideas swirl and
spin. In emptiness is
everything. The light is
there; it's trickling in.
A light that travels
deep within. Existing
in each living being.
The light of dreams
and dreams of light
that dance upon
the navy night.
I'm trying to tell
you how it is –
The use of time
is up to us.
The time is NOW,
such pure delight.
To spend your time
just how you like.

It's Me, The Fly

Zippee, Zappah,
It's me the fly!
I don't care if
I live or die.

I'll zip your ear,
I'll zap your eye.
Zippee, Zappah,
it's me the fly!

I zoom by food
and snatch a bite,
it's a bizzy life,
I'm a bizzy guy.

I'm in the fridge,
on the apple pie,
Zippee, Zappah,
it's me the fly!

I'm on the worktop,
at the bread,
I'm still alive,
you want me dead!

I'll zig zag laps
around your head.
I'll fill your world
with dread.

Zippee, Zappah,
it's me the fly!
I'm sure you'll be
quite horrified

To know that I
survived the night.
Another day.
Another fight!

Fire

Fire
will take
all that it
must. Strip an
object down to
dust. Give it
fuel and give
it heat. Give it
oxygen and see.
Fire will snatch away
the living. Fire is hungry.
U n f o r g i v i n g

Duck's Final Day

It's never nice,
is it? But I suppose
all that lives must
eventually go.

Having said that though.
If a duck could choose
the last day of its life.
It would probably do
something pleasant like;

Eat some worms
and fall asleep.
Then float away in a
drizzly dream.

Or waddle and doddle
to a bug-filled puddle,
gobble all the bugs
and die without trouble.

But the duck in
question was killed
by a buzzard.
Nothing fancy.
No ketchup or mustard.

His friends watched
in horror with nothing
to say. And that's all I
know of the duck's final day.

From The Folly

The first spin of day
from the Folly. The tower.
The watcher. Watching over
yellow and green and quiet
fields. Homes and barns,
sleepy heads. Mist clinging
to the grooves of land.
Sun glowing through dusty
clouds. Round and red.
The Folly. Absorbing it all.
From this high hill octagon.
A hot air balloon on the horizon.
Hawthorn sprinkling the hedgerows.
The dog and I, listening to the
powdery sky. Listening to the
busy lives, the little cars with
little lights like little stars.
A brand-new day, a brand-new
dream. To dance and
sing and think and breathe.
To laugh and cry, to question why.
From the Folly, I watch the world
go by.

The Folly Tower of Pontypool was demolished during WWII to avoid it serving as an aerial landmark for opposition bombers. A successful campaign by the charity C.R.O.F.T. (Campaign to rebuild the Old Folly Tower) saw it rebuilt in 1994. On a clear day, you can view seven surrounding counties. Pontypool is a small valley town in south-east Wales.

Friendship

The beauty of friendship,
the people we find,
they enter our lives
at the sweetest times.

As simple as sunrise,
bright as the moon,
you smile upon me,
and I smile upon you.

They say what's meant for you
will not pass you by,
so I thank you for
shining your light.

For rising and beaming
like stars in the sky.
For us being together,
side by side.

For growing together
like flowers in bloom.
For flowing like water,
in rhythm, in tune.

The beauty of friendship,
the people we find,
they enter our lives
at the sweetest times.

I wrote this poem for my dear friends at UCAN productions (Unique Creative Arts Network) A creative arts charity for blind and partially sighted children, young people, adults and their friends. Based in Cardiff, Wales.

Dreadlock Dragon

Yea, I'm a dragon,
but I'm a rockstar too,
it's hard to separate the two.

I wear black shades
and I've got tattoos,
I don't fit in. I break the rules!

I'm a one-off, an icon,
the Dreadlock Dragon –
I make music, man. It's my passion.

I set trends, high fashion,
just bought me a mansion,
my album New Flame went platinum.

I don't take selfies.
I never smile. I've got my
own vibe, my own style.

Dragon punk, hot rocker,
sharp claws, chart topper,
off the scale, sky-high,
super cool, super fly!

Dear Human

It's sticky to say this,
I mean tricky!
But the crisps and the sweeties
have got me all greasy!
I mean seriously buddy,
What the heck. Why can't
you show me some respect!
I'm the channel changer,
the clicker, the clacker –
the gadget, the gizmo
the doofer, the zapper –
but you don't see any
of that. I'm overlooked
it's a FACT!
By the time that you read
this, I'll be on the run!
Living with you is a
pain in the bum!
I deserve so much better –
I deserve to be free.
Good luck finding something
to watch without me.

Yours Sincerely

The Runaway Remote.

P.S From someone who's been
lost beneath the settee,
it could do with a hoover,
at least once a week!

The Punchbowl

Hot day dry day
tall grass sway sway,
nettle fern and
foxglove play play.
Down the hill
on dusty tracks,
crunchy leaves
and twigs that crack.
One step two step
tickling nearer,
soon the watery sight
is clearer.
Gently rippling,
surface glittering,
somewhere close
the crows are
bickering. Chittering
chattering, sheep are
nattering. Sunshine on
the hill is mellowing.
Past the hay bales,
trees with tall tales.
Past the frog and
evening-stroll snails.
Quiet and sweet
with gentle feet.
There's a deer in

the meadow if you
take a peek. There's
a distant mountain
fast asleep. And
clouds piled up in
sugary heaps.
Then up the hill
and softly over.
Hazel, beach and
four leaf clover.
Hot day dry day
tall grass sway sway,
nettle fern and
foxglove play play.

'The Punchbowl' is the name of a lovely lake near my home. A hidden lake. Nestled between the trees. A special place.

Horse on the Highway

Now this is hard to say,
but I'll tell you anyway.
A horse stole my car,
and sped towards the highway!

First, he filled the boot with hay,
and yelled I'm going on a journey!
Not In my car! I cried,
but he replied, just try and stop me!

Farmyard radio to the max,
he's singing E-I-E-I-O.
Wheel spinning off my driveway,
and zig-zagging down the road.

With a beep beep here
and a vroom vroom there,
head through the sunroof
and wind in his hair.

One hoof at the gas,
one hoof at the gear,
two hooves at the wheel,
police cars at the rear!

And it's prime-time news,
the whole nation is glued
to the horse on the highway
singing farmyard tunes.

No one knows his destination
but he's become a superstar!
I just wish he'd pulled this stunt,
in my next-door NAYbour's car!

In my second book of poetry Doughnuts, Thieves and Chimpanzees, there is a poem called 'Horse On The Loo'. And yes, that's right, a horse thought it would be a good idea to use my toilet, my loo! In case you are wondering, YES, it's the very same horse! What on earth will he do next?

Bramble

Will rip and tear
at the shin. Pull
blood from the skin.
Nature's NO ENTRY sign.
Turn back, it says,
or get sliced,
scrammed and hooked.
It's a horrible hullabaloo
to be wrapped up in
their sharp cling.
Caught up in a thick
thorn sting. But bramble
has a tasty offering.
Carefully does it,
gentle, gentle.
Blackberries growing
ornamental.
Blackberries brimmed
with beaming light.
Juicy jungle,
blackberry crumble.
Squishy squashy,
yummy yum.
Picking berries one
by one. Fill the belly,
fill the tubs. Ignoring
beetles, bugs and grubs.

I’ve told you now,
so DO BEWARE!
Of the bramble’s warning,
the prickly scare!
But don’t forget their
fruity flare. You’ll never
know if you never dare!

Welsh Wolf

There is a wild wolf
wandering the Welsh hills.
The last wolf. Grinning and
growling at the villages below.
Those twinkling lights, shining like
the wolf's teeth in moonlight.
Of course, he snatches things
to stay alive. For a hungry-eyed
hunter, the menu is delightful.
Anything flesh and bone.
It's hard to know when a
wolf is watching.
The wolf will watch for as long
as it takes. Hours, days.
But never weeks.
No. The wolf will watch
your whereabouts.
That evening stroll to the shop.
The quick trip to your nan's.
And then, when you are

walking home, the wolf will
smell the flesh and bone.
The stage is right,
the moon is bright.

A. Wolf ends your life,
with a single bite!

B. Wolf ate too much,
you're safe tonight.

C. Wolf howls into
the lonely night.

There are multiple endings for the poem.
You can choose whichever suits. But you should know, only one of them is true.

Magnus Mole

Oh hello,
it's Magnus Mole.
Don't mind me, just digging holes!
Well, tunnels in fact, to be precise.
And I find your garden rather nice.
I'm here and there as you can tell.
The views from here are swell.
Your soil is good; it's rich and healthy.
Earthworms, slugs and grubs a plenty!
Tell you what chap, I'll show you around.
Just marvel at all my lovely mounds.
With soily walls and soily ground,
It's jolly great! I'll stick around.
Goodbye ol' chum, it's been a blaast.
When having fun, time sure goes faast.
Now off you pop, it's past my tea.
One values one's own privacy.

Blackbird

Blackbird bouncing
on the woodpile. Waking
up nothing. Stump to stump.
Quietly, quietly. Then down
to the ground. A leaf pile.
Noisier now. Yellow beak
tossing the leaves.
Rummaging for wriggly
things. Happy worms.
Unsuspecting. From the
frosty earth to the warmer
insides of the blackbird's belly.

Stone Wall

I'm near the stone wall at the edge of the woods. Those moss-covered stones that glow green when the sun is low and leaping through leaf and shadow. This, I suppose, is what the wall knows. Weathering it all. Raindrop and snowfall. Summertime sun wall, collecting crow calls and other country things. Like weasels weaving the slim space, and watching out as the world hides at the warning of red sky in the morning, where twilight tickles fear into the minds of the living. What isn't bubbling over is brewing under. And somewhere in the thick slick mix of bad and good. I'm near the stone wall, at the edge of the woods.

In The Land of Music

In the land of music, everything has a tune,
dubstep in drainpipes and bins singing blues.

We beatbox for breakfast and disco for dinner,
techno for tea and samba for supper.

When daylight dances into dark,
the sky is sweet with singing harps.

When darkness sweeps away the day,
pianos play then fade away.

There are no Tyrones only Trombones,
no Monicas but Harmonicas.

The nation's favourite baby names
are Banjo and Melodica.

The rivers, hills and swaying trees
are humming humble harmonies.

The cats and dogs are singing folk,
the bats and frogs sing songs of hope.

Ballads and baritones, tempo and key,
watery whistles from whales under sea.

In the land of music, everything has a tune.
From the sweet singing sun to melodious moon.

Giddy Life

I love this giddy life,
where poems rattle
around my brain and
brighten up my day.
Where ideas dance
and groove and slide
into the magic of my mind.

It's a charmed life it's true,
everyday a chance
at something new.
Each day a precious gift,
I'm alive, I exist!
I'll carve my own reality
and give the world
the best of me.

Fuzzy Foot

By fuzzy foot,
I mean, a foot that's
gone all … f u z z y.
It's a weird feeling,
ticklish, sensitive, numb!
Do you recognise this awful
sensation I'm talking about?
Fuzzy kinda makes it sound nice.
IT'S NOT NICE!
I'm not talking about
pins and needles
though it can lead to that –
And I don't know which is worse.
What I do know is this,
I cannot walk with fuzzy foot.
And sometimes it travels further
up the leg. I try to shake it off.
THAT DOESN'T WORK!
So I just wait, and hope that
maybe one day I'll get my
foot back. The foot I once
knew and loved.

AI

AI won't stop me writing, No!
I write because I love it so.

AI can write things brilliantly, yes.
But I do ME the best!

Imagine not climbing because
monkeys exist.

Imagine not swimming because
dolphins exist.

Imagine leaving all fun to comedians,
it's a daft idea is this!

Creating is endless, an open sky,
there's room for all of us to fly.

AI as a tool enhances you.
It will challenge and develop you.

And what you choose to ask of it,
determines how you benefit.

Don't shy away or be afraid,
the joy of making never fades.

Hold tight to passion, wonder, pleasure.
Searching, scratching, finding treasure.

Ghost

Even the word has
something spooky about it. Ghost.
it's even spookier without
the capital G.   ghost.
Thing is, I have no proof that
they actually exist. No solid
evidence. They say ghosts have
unfinished business. Like what exactly?
A game of monopoly that nobody won?
Or that leaky sink they promised to
fix but never did?
Sometimes in a dream or nightmare, I
walk around the place, I do random stuff
and it all feels real, very real. Am I ghost
then? Has a part of me left my body
intentionally – to join another world, to search
for truths that cannot be found
by those who are awake, living. Only
the drifters, drifting. Only spirits, souls,
Ghouls and ghosts. The crossover, who
really knows...
                    Hold on a moment,
I can't be sure, but I think someone
just knocked my door. After midnight –
that's pretty rare. I go to check, but
no one's there. It knocks again, but louder
now. The cat shrieks a strange meow.

The door begins to open up, I run
towards and slam it shut! But then
a window opens wide – and darkness
snakes its way inside. And sounds
in shadows that creep and crawl and cling
to things along the hall. A voice perhaps,
some ghostly mutter. I ask 'who's there?'
with a trembling stutter.
The weight of darkness on my back.
The weight of worry pins me flat!
And soon before my very eyes,
a shape emerges from the night,
A figure edging close to me,
I cannot blink. I cannot breathe!
I cannot think. I cannot speak!
Then goodness grief!
BEEP beep BEEP beep –

My alarm bell shakes me
from my sleep!

Cross Country

I'm enjoying the light.
Low light. Glowing the
lonely barns as I pass.
I glide by on the train.
Float by. Flashes of
fields through the
tree line. Sleepy
passengers settle
down. Snuggle
into the slow time.
Twilight. Big sky.
And then there is
water. And then
there is not.
A tunnel takes
most of it away.
But not sound.
Through the hill's
deep stomach and
out again, on the
other side. How
green the grass
looks. How blue
the sky.

Jetting Off

Here we go.
Lifting off.
Leaving all that
I know on the
ground. I'm jetting
off to engine sounds.
With giant wings
that balance things,
in the high sky
where a fly would
freeze. Above the
clouds and overseas.
For a metal bird,
it's quite a breeze,
to float at thirty
thousand feet.

The World's an Adventure!

Listen to sounds as they leap wall to wall,
see rainbows in the mist of waterfalls,
make friends with the mouse in the dusty old boot,
the world's an adventure it's true.

When puddles are brave, they grow into lakes,
garden flowers grow legs and tiptoe to escape,
the sky turns pink to shake off the blues,
the world's an adventure it's true.

Build castles from sand with your bare hands,
make pools in a river with sticks as a dam,
there's plenty to do when you follow the clues,
the world's an adventure it's true.

Kindness is a gift you get back in return,
see how the sun and moon take turns,
birds sing and flowers bloom all for you,
the world's an adventure it's true,
the world's an adventure it's true.

Spider

In my shed. There
is a spider. I never
know just where it'll be
but I know it's eyes
are on me. It's big,
suspiciously big!
Thick legs and a
thick body. It lives in
darkness. When I
open the door and
light gets in. I see it.
Wrapping up another
spider in rough silk.
Thick silk. Makes a
mummy of it! Steals
away its last breath.
I close the door.
And I know that in the
darkness. It will gobble
it all up. Every piece.
And then grow outwards.
Bursting from its skin.
Into something larger.
Something hungrier
than before.

It's Me, the Flea

Haha Hehe,
it's me the flea,
I'm never heard
and seldom seen.

But when I bite
you'll know it's me,
Haha Hehe,
it's me the flea.

I'm on the dog,
the rent is free,
I'm travelling
with my family,

I'll hop off
onto your settee,
Haha Hehe,
it's me the flea.

It's cosy here,
I cannot lie,
the perfect place
to multiply!

I bring the scritch,
I bring the scratch,

then I watch my
children hatch.

Haha Hehe,
it's me the flea,
I've settled in
successfully.

Dreadfully and
recklessly.
My parents will be
proud of me!

The Truth

The Truth can
live in shadow.
A murky mystery.
And even when
It comes to light
some choose not
to believe. But truth
makes way for space
to dream. Truth is a bird,
wide winged and free.

It Will Fall Again As Rain

it will fall again as rain

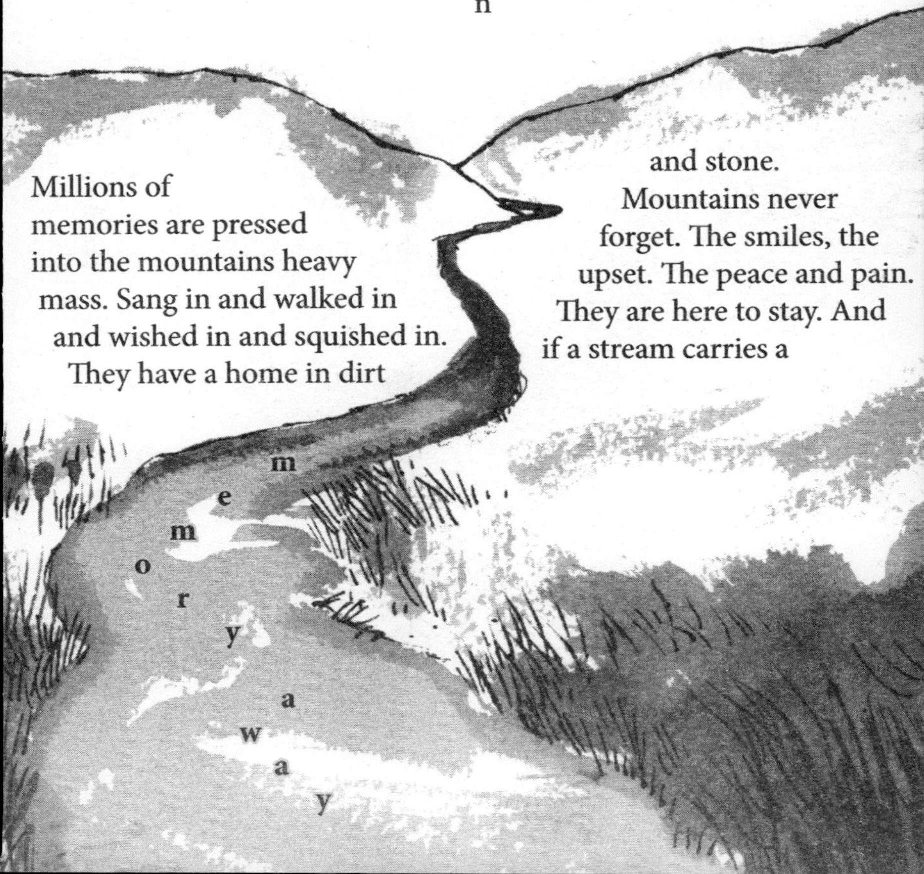

Millions of
memories are pressed
into the mountains heavy
mass. Sang in and walked in
and wished in and squished in.
They have a home in dirt
and stone.
Mountains never
forget. The smiles, the
upset. The peace and pain.
They are here to stay. And
if a stream carries a
memory away

All Night

I stay awake all night
hanging out with bats,
circling the lamp posts,
slinking in shadows.

I stay awake all night
hanging out with cats,
on my dainty tippy-toes
I go wherever the cats go.

I stay awake all night
hanging out with dogs,
barking at the moon,
then I sleep all afternoon.

I stay awake all night
because I'm afraid of the dark.
Out there I hear noises,
out there, dogs bark,
out there, bats circle,
out there, cats are creeping,
out there is everything –
that I do, when I'm dreaming.

Poetry Crime

The poems have gone,
there's nothing there.
Not good for a poet,
a terrible scare!

No haikus, couplets
rhythm or rhyme,
I feel I'm at the scene
of a poetry crime!

A poetry pirate!
A scoundrel, a thief.
Snatching my words,
it beggars belief!

Inspector, Detective,
pick up the phone!
Locate my poems,
bring them back home.

Home

The way the winds on
the west coast of Wales sing.
And the mystical forests
collect midnight calls of owl.
Scatty flight paths of bat,
and the thunderclaps
of a waterfall.
Water into water.

I know of this rock,
steel and coal.
I know of streams that
swallow sunbeams and
tickle stone with starlight
twinkling. The trees are
listening; they are leaning in.

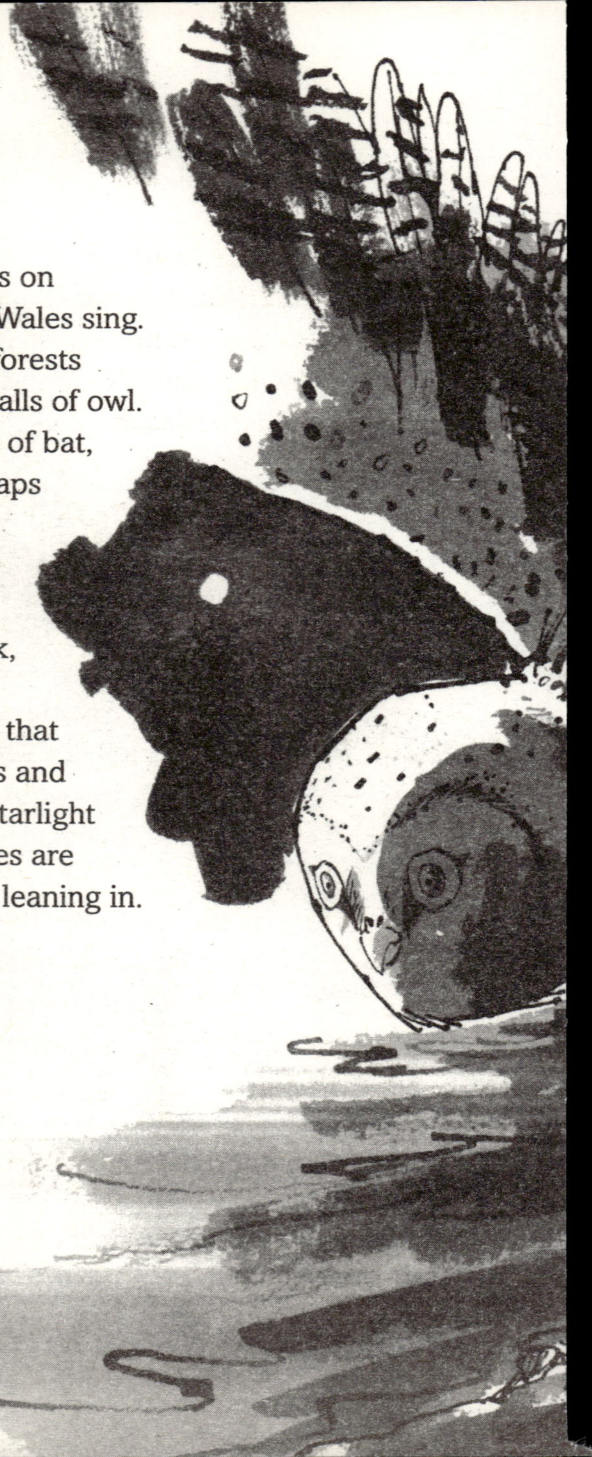

This land is a collection
of feelings, absorbed
and told again.
Poems born into flowers,
tales sewn into leaf,
memories embedded in
the mind of the mountain.
And dreams that whisper
from the silver sea.

Praise for Alex's work

Red Sky at Night, Poet's Delight: Illustrated by Ian Morris

'A beautiful little collection that packs a punch! Infinitely readable and shareable poems to make you smile, reflect and dream.'
Rashmi Sirdeshpande

Selected for the Summer Reading Challenge

Daydreams and Jellybeans: Illustrated by Katy Riddell

'This is a lovely, warm collection of poems that hail from a place of wonder and mystery.' Joshua Segal

Shortlisted for the Wales Book of the Year and the Lollies Laugh-out Loud Awards

***Doughnuts, Thieves and Chimpanzees*:**
Illustrated by Rhiannon Smith

'A joyous dive into poetry.' Joseph Coelho

Nominated for the Yoto Carnegie Medal 2025